នៅភូមិខ្ញុំ

In My Village

By
Lauren Iida & Carolyn R. Hall

Illustrated by
Cherylin Andre, Lauren Armstrong, JD Banke, Carolyn R. Hall, Lauren Iida, Heather Elder, Karina Nyquist, Aimee Oberstein, Bradley Taylor

Dedicated to
the children of Prasot village
Svay Rieng, Cambodia

នៅភូមិខ្ញុំ ពេលព្រឹកព្រះអាទិត្យតែងតែរះចែងចាំង
ភ្លឺស្រឡះ មនុស្សម្នាអ៊ូអរ មាន់រងាវ-កុកកឹកតៗ!
ហើយឆ្កែតែងតែព្រុះ។ នៅភូមិខ្ញុំ អ្នកជិតខាង
ច្រៀងខារ៉ាអូខេនៅពេលព្រឹក -ឡាឡាឡាឡាឡា។
នៅភូមិខ្ញុំ ពេលព្រឹកតែងតែមានរឿងយ៉ាងដូច្នេះ។

In my village, the morning always comes.

It is bright and noisy,

the rooster crows — cock-a-doodle-doo!

And the dogs always bark.

In my village, the neighbor sings karaoke in the morning — la la la la la.

In my village, the morning always comes.

នៅភូមិខ្ញុំ យើងតែងតែបង្កាត់ភ្លើង។ ភ្លើងក្តៅមានពណ៌
ក្រហមឆេះ និងពណ៌ទឹកក្រូចភ្លឺ។ ឮសំឡេងរប៉េះរប៉ោះ
ហើយពេលខ្លះ មានអណ្តាតភ្លើងពណ៌ខៀវតិចៗ។
នៅពេលព្រឹក យើងដាំទឹកសម្រាប់ដាក់តែ និង
ចម្អិនអាហារ។ នៅពេលយប់ ផ្សែងភ្លើងការពារ
ក្របីឃ្លៀចដែលកំពុងដេកកុំឲ្យមូសខាំ។ នៅភូមិខ្ញុំ
តែងមានផុតភ្លើងយ៉ាងកក់ក្តៅ។

In my village, we make fires.

They are hot and bright and burn red and orange.

They snap and crackle, and sometimes there are tiny blue flames.

In the morning, we boil water for tea and cooking.

At night, the smoke protects the sleeping water buffalo from mosquitos.

In my village, the fires are hot.

នៅភូមិខ្ញុំ មានត្រពាំងមួយដែលក្មេងៗចូលចិត្តចាប់ត្រី
នឹងអង្រុត់។ ទឹកត្រពាំងបានមកពីទឹកភ្លៀង។ ត្រីអណ្ដែង
អន្ទង់ ក្ដាម និងកង្កែបរស់នៅក្នុងត្រពាំង។ ក្របីឃ្លៀចលេង
ទឹកភក់ត្រជាក់។ ទឹកភ្លឺព្រិចៗនៅពេលព្រឹក និង
មានសភាពស្ងប់នៅពេលយប់។ នៅភូមិខ្ញុំ មានត្រពាំងមួយ
ដែលក្មេងៗចូលចិត្តចាប់ត្រី។

In my village, there is a pond where the children catch fish with baskets.

The pond is made of rain water —

catfish, eels, crabs, and frogs live in the pond.

Water buffalo wade in the cool mud.

The water twinkles in the morning and is still at night.

In my village, there is a pond where the children fish.

នៅភូមិខ្ញុំ ផ្កាឈូកជះក្លិនស្រស់ស្រាយ។
ផ្កាឈូកមានពណ៌ស៊ីជម្ពូរ និងបៃតង ហើយដុះក្នុងត្រពាំង
។ សត្វកន្ទុំរុយទំលើផ្កាឈូក កង្កែបអង្គុយលើស្លឹកឈូក។
យើងញ៉ាំក្រអៅឈូកស្រួយ និងបេះផ្កាឈូកថ្វាយព្រះ។
នៅភូមិខ្ញុំ ផ្កាឈូកធុំក្លិនក្រអូប។

In my village, the lotus smells fresh.

The flowers are pink and green, and they grow in the pond.

Dragonflies land on the flowers,

and frogs sit on the leaves.

We eat the crunchy stalks

and take the flowers to the temple.

In my village, the lotus smells sweet.

នៅភូមិខ្ញុំ យើងញ៉ាំបាយរាល់ថ្ងៃ។ យើងញ៉ាំបាយជាមួយ
នឹងត្រី។ ហើយយើងញ៉ាំបាយជាមួយសម្ល
យើងញ៉ាំបាយជាមួយស្លៃប៉ាក់ឆយ ដំឡូងជ្វា និងស្លៃ។
យើងញ៉ាំបាយដំណើបជាមួយស្វាយជាបង្អែម។ នៅភូមិខ្ញុំ
យើងដាំស្រូវ និងទទួលទានបាយជារៀងរាល់ថ្ងៃ។

In my village, we eat rice every day.

We eat it with fish,

and we eat it with soup.

We eat it with bok choy, sweet potatoes, and cabbage.

We eat sticky rice with mangoes for dessert.

In my village, we grow rice and we eat it every day.

នៅភូមិខ្ញុំ យើងពាក់ស្បែកជើងផ្ទាត់។ ស្បែកជើងផ្ទាត់របស់យើងធ្វើពីកៅស៊ូ និងមានគ្រប់ទំហំ។ មានពណ៌ខៀវ ពណ៌ស ឬពណ៌ខ្មៅ។ យើងពាក់ស្បែកផ្ទាត់រត់លើគ្រួសទៅសាលារៀន ហើយយើងទិញខ្ញី ស្ករស គ្រឿងទេស និងម្ទេសពីផ្សារមកដាក់ផ្ទះ។ នៅភូមិខ្ញុំ យើងពាក់ស្បែកជើងផ្ទាត់។

In my village, we wear flip-flops on our feet.

Our flip-flops are made of rubber, and they come in every size.

They are blue or white or black.

In our flip-flops, we run fast over rocks to school,

and we carry ginger, sugar, spices, and chilies home from the market.

In my village, we wear flip-flops on our feet.

នៅភូមិខ្ញុំ ក្របីឃ្លៀចមានកម្លាំងខ្លាំង។ ក្របីមាន
ស្នែងកោងហើយវែង មានពាក់កន្លុះនឹងច្រមុះ និងទម្ងន់
១០០០ គីឡូក្រាម។ នៅភូមិខ្ញុំ គេប្រើក្របីឃ្លៀចភ្ជួរស្រែ
ដឹកម្រះ ជីវ៉ាន់ស៊ុយ សណ្ដែកហាឡាំងតាវតាមរទេះ។
គេក៏ប្រើក្របីឃ្លៀចដើម្បីដឹកសម្ភារផ្សេងៗ និងដឹកមនុស្ស
ផងដែរ។ នៅពេលយប់ ក្របីឃ្លៀចដេកក្នុងក្រោល។

In my village, the water buffalo is strong.

She has long curved horns, a rope through her nose, and she weighs 1,000 kilograms.

In my village, the water buffalo plows the rice field.

She carries bitter melons, cilantro, and snow peas in her cart —

she also carries tools and people.

At night, the water buffalo sleeps in the barn.

In my village, the water buffalo is strong.

នៅភូមិខ្ញុំ ក្របីឃ្មៀចមានកម្លាំងខ្លាំង។ នៅភូមិខ្ញុំ ក្មេងៗ
មានខ្មៅដៃ។ ខ្មៅដៃធ្វើពីឈើ និងមានបណ្តូលខ្មៅដៃ
មានជ័រលុបពណ៌ស៊ីជម្ពូរ។ យើងខួងខ្មៅដៃឲ្យមុត
ហើយវាកាន់តែខ្លីទៅមុខ។ យើងប្រើខ្មៅដៃដើម្បីគូររូបភាព
គូសវាស និងសរសេររឿង។ ពេលខ្លះ យើងសរសេរ
សំបុត្រទៅមិត្តភក្តិ និងចុះហត្ថលេខា។ នៅភូមិខ្ញុំ
ក្មេងៗមានខ្មៅដៃ ហើយខ្មៅដៃនេះគឺសម្រាប់អ្នក!

In my village, the children have pencils.

The pencils are made of wood and lead and have a pink eraser.

We sharpen them and they grow short.

We draw pictures, scribble, and write stories.

Sometimes we write letters to our friends and sign our names.

In my village, the children have pencils.

នៅភូមិខ្ញុំ យើងមានសៀវភៅ។ យើងបើកគម្រប និង
ទំព័រសៀវភៅ។ យើងអានអក្សរ និងមើលរូបភាព។
ពេលខ្លះ យើងអានឲ្យបងប្អូនប្រុសស្រីយើងស្តាប់។
យើងអាចសរសេរនៅក្នុងសៀវភៅផ្ទាល់ខ្លួនរបស់យើង
ផងដែរ។ នៅភូមិខ្ញុំ យើងមានសៀវភៅ។

In my village, we have books.

We open their covers and turn the pages.

We read the words and look at the pictures.

Sometimes we read to our brothers and sisters.

We can write our own books too.

In my village, we have books.

tiny apartment. But
of course
her lifetime
of an attractively set
bride should

នៅភូមិខ្ញុំ ភាពងងឹតគ្របដណ្តប់នាពេលរាត្រី។ ផ្កាយ និង
ព្រះច័ន្ទរះបំភ្លឺពេលរាត្រី។ ពេលយប់អាកាសធាតុត្រជាក់។
យើងស្តាប់ឮសំឡេងចង្រិតយំ និងសំឡេងកង្កែប។
ពេលខ្លះយើងអានសៀវភៅនៅពេលយប់។ នៅភូមិខ្ញុំ
ពេលព្រឹកព្រលឹមថ្ងៃរះចែងចាំងស្មើតែងតែមកជំនួសរាត្រី
អន្ធិការដែលរំលងផុតទៅ។

In my village, the night is dark.

The stars come out and the moon glows.

The night is cool.

We listen to the crickets and frogs.

Sometimes at night we read our books.

In my village, the bright morning always follows the dark night.

The End

About This Book

The Antipodes Collective was founded in 2014 by Lauren Iida, a Seattle artist and graduate of Cornish College of the Arts. Over several years of working in Cambodia as a social entrepreneur and volunteer, Iida noticed a vast need for learning materials that were culturally relevant to Khmer children.

Due to the decimation of literary, visual, and performing arts by Pol Pot's Khmer Rouge regime in the 1970s, there are relatively few Khmer-focused children's books available.

Connecting her Seattle arts community with her interest in effective educational tools for Cambodian students, The Antipodes Collective came to fruition. The organization creates quality learning materials to captivate, educate, and inspire children through the elevation of their own lives.

Profits from the sale of this book go directly to supporting the children's literacy and arts projects of The Antipodes Collective.

www.theantipodescollective.org

"Morning" cut paper by Lauren Iida
www.laureniida.com

"Fire" smoke, watercolor on paper by Cherylin Andre
www.cherylinandre.com

"Pond" gouache on paper by Heather Elder
www.leadfeatherstudio.com

"Lotus" collage by Carolyn R. Hall
www.carolynrhallwriter.com

"Rice" cut paper by Lauren Iida

"Flip Flop" acrylic on paper by JD Banke
www.jdbanke.squarespace.com

"Water Buffalo" ink, watercolor on paper by Lauren Armstrong
www.tigerchildrencobramountain.com

"Pencil" digital drawing by Karina Nyquist
www.karinanyquist.com

"Book" acrylic on wood panel by Aimee Oberstein
www.leabela.com

"Night" woodblock on paper by Bradley Taylor
www.bradleytaylorart.com

Special thanks to
Mary Matsuda Gruenewald
Linda Ando
San Sambo
Lucy Mohl
Jennifer Pletsch
Koji Minami
Sally the Cat

Made in the USA
San Bernardino, CA
13 July 2018